A Baker's Portrait

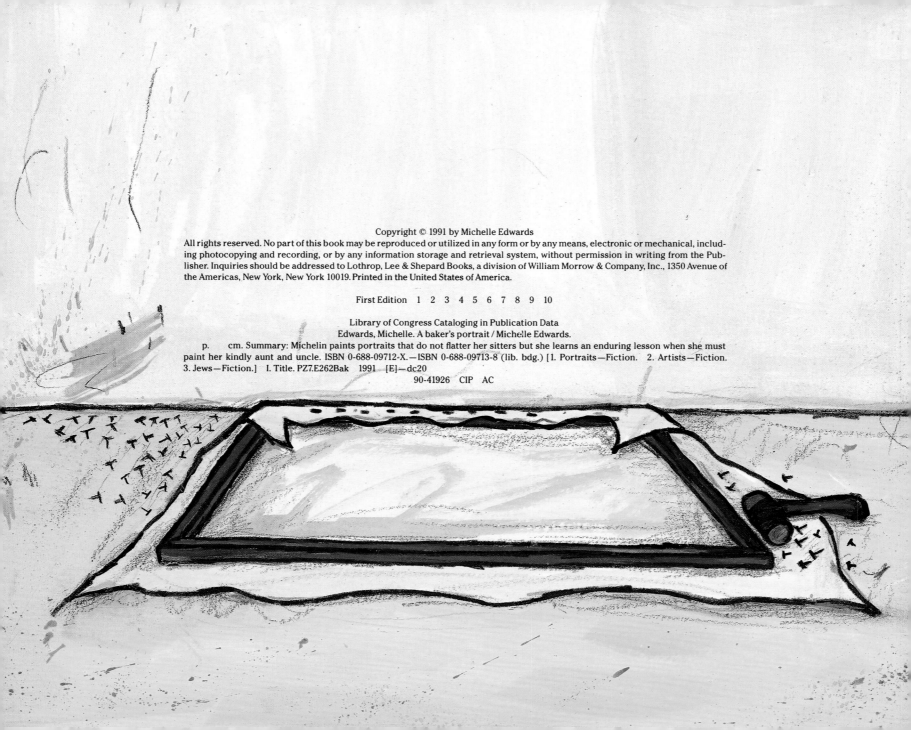

First Edition   1   2   3   4   5   6   7   8   9   10

Library of Congress Cataloging in Publication Data
Edwards, Michelle. A baker's portrait / Michelle Edwards.
p.   cm. Summary: Michelin paints portraits that do not flatter her sitters but she learns an enduring lesson when she must paint her kindly aunt and uncle. ISBN 0-688-09712-X.—ISBN 0-688-09713-8 (lib. bdg.) [1. Portraits—Fiction.   2. Artists—Fiction.   3. Jews—Fiction.]   I. Title. PZ7.E262Bak   1991   [E]—dc20
90-41926 CIP AC

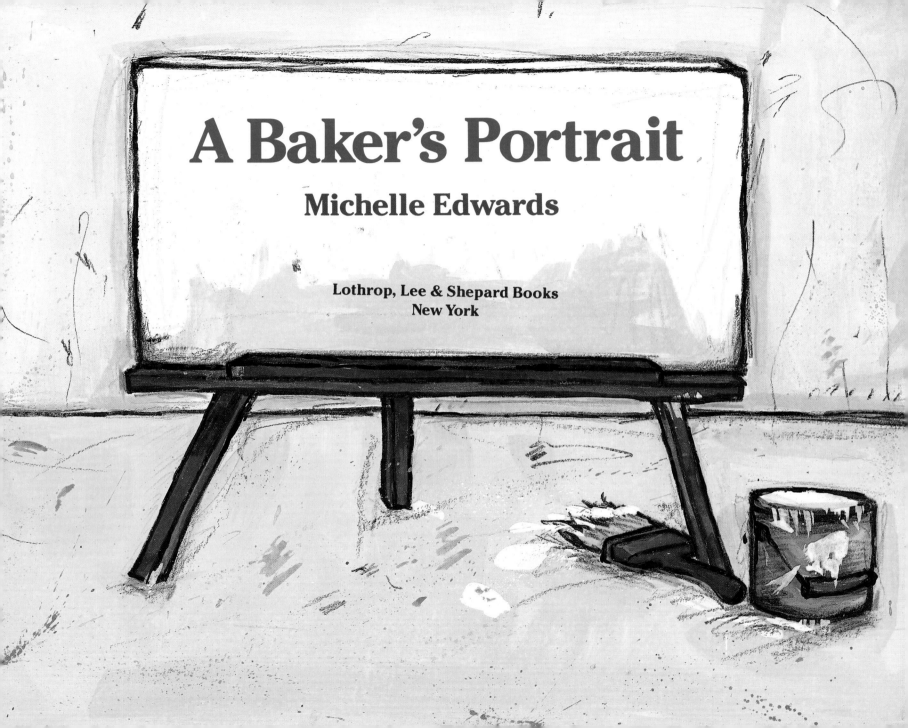

A Baker's Portrait

Michelle Edwards

Lothrop, Lee & Shepard Books
New York

In the town of Hoshel, after the leaves had fallen from the trees and the farmers had prepared for a long winter's rest, a portrait painter named Michelin sat in her studio and sulked.

There hadn't been much business for Michelin since she'd painted the mayor of Alaga and his family. Michelin always painted just what she saw. And when she saw the fat mayor, his warty wife, and their cross-eyed children, she looked very carefully at them, and then painted just what she saw.

"So what would be so terrible if you didn't paint every wart on her face?" Grandma Levy asked her one day. "Couldn't you give someone a little enjoyment? Make someone happy? Make someone beautiful?"

"Think about what she says," said Mama. "Because a little business has come your way. Your beloved Aunt Liliane and Uncle Ferdinand want you to paint their portraits."

Michelin's stomach ached. Ferdinand and Liliane were bakers. They were so fat, they broke chairs. When Beauty had knocked on *their* door, they must have been kneading bread.

"Tomorrow you start," Grandma Levy told her. "And you will stay with Ferdinand and Liliane until the portraits are finished."

The next afternoon, Ferdinand and Liliane greeted Michelin at the back door. They were even fatter than she had remembered.

"So, my lovely niece, how and when do we begin?" asked Aunt Liliane with a big smile. Michelin had forgotten that all of her bottom teeth were missing.

"First I need some time to think," Michelin told them.

Michelin went upstairs to the big room Ferdinand and Liliane had given to her. She set up her easel and her paints, but all she could think about were Ferdinand's big belly and Liliane's missing teeth.

Michelin imagined her aunt and uncle as king and queen of their bakery, in beautiful white aprons and crowning white bakers' hats. But when she drew their faces, they turned out just like Ferdinand and Liliane, ordinary bakers, fat and ugly.

"Perhaps tomorrow will be better," said Michelin before she went to sleep.

The next morning, and every morning after, Michelin drew. After a few weeks, she had piles and piles of drawings. Drawings of Ferdinand with hair he hadn't had for years. Drawings of Ferdinand without any hair at all. Drawings of Liliane with a mouthful of teeth. Drawings of her without top teeth or bottoms. Drawings that were terrible. Drawings that would make Ferdinand and Liliane scream, not to mention what Grandma Levy might do.

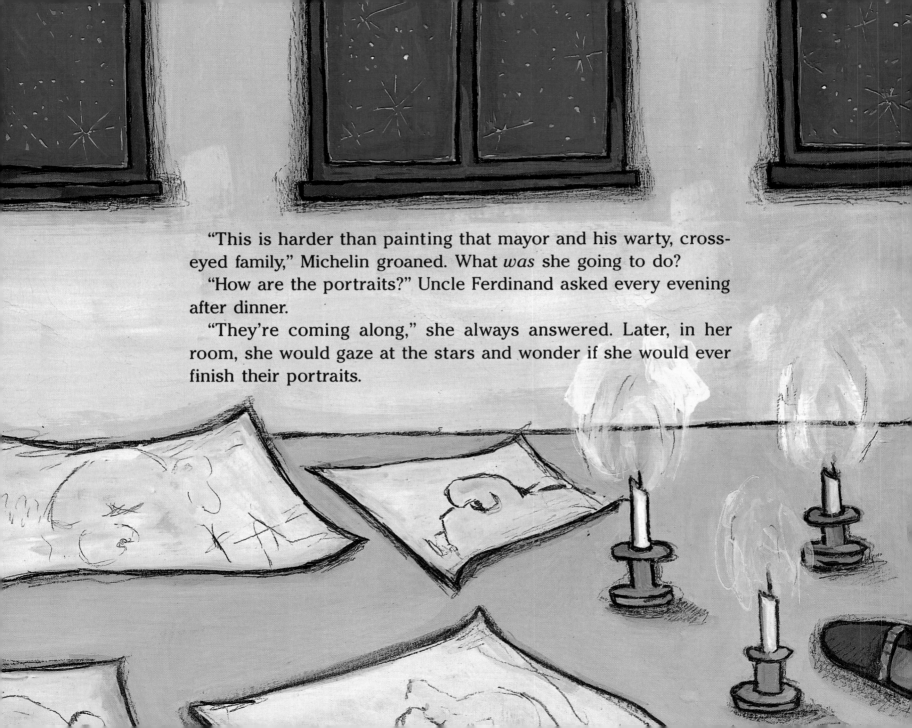

"This is harder than painting that mayor and his warty, cross-eyed family," Michelin groaned. What *was* she going to do?

"How are the portraits?" Uncle Ferdinand asked every evening after dinner.

"They're coming along," she always answered. Later, in her room, she would gaze at the stars and wonder if she would ever finish their portraits.

Then one evening, Uncle Ferdinand knocked on her door.

"I thought you might like another piece of chocolate cake," he said as he plopped down in a big old chair. "You know, Michelin, when I look at that cake, I think of my Lili. Sweet on the outside and rich on the inside.

"Sometimes we joke, Lili and me. I tell her she's my chocolate cake. She tells me I'm her challah—a little crusty on the outside, but soft on the inside. And you know, Michelin," Uncle Ferdinand whispered, "no matter how old the challah, it always tastes as good as the day it was baked."

After Uncle Ferdinand left the room, Michelin stared at the cake for a long time. Then she took a canvas from the corner, put it on her easel, and began to paint. She painted all night long.

The next morning, Michelin flew down the stairs and ran into the kitchen. "Your portraits are done!" she shouted.

Ferdinand and Liliane rushed into town to tell everyone that the moment had finally arrived. Soon friends and relatives began pouring into their house.

Uncle Lev the barber and his wife, Sonya, and their six children came.

Cousin Sarah the butcher and her husband, Lazar, came.

Rabbi Raffi and his wife, Hannah, and their new baby, Isaac, came.

And finally Mama came with Grandma Levy.

"How much longer must an old lady wait?" growled Grandma
Levy. "Bring down your masterpiece."

Michelin ran to her room, threw a sheet over her painting,
carried it downstairs, and set it up in the middle of the room.

Suddenly, everyone was quiet.

Rabbi Raffi said a prayer.

Ferdinand and Liliane closed their eyes and held hands. With
Michelin's portraits one never knew.

Then, holding her breath, Michelin lifted the sheet.

"Lili, my chocolate cake!" cried Uncle Ferdinand. "It is really us!" He gave Aunt Liliane a big kiss.

Aunt Liliane began to cry. "Oh, Ferdie. You crusty old challah. Isn't it wonderful!"

Everyone crowded around the painting.

"What did I tell you, Lili?" exclaimed Mama. "My daughter is another da Vinci."

"From you I never expected such a thing," barked Grandma Levy. "Other things maybe, but not this." She patted Michelin's arm. "Now you are ready. Now I shall let you paint *my* portrait."

Michelin looked into the pale blue of Grandma Levy's beady eyes. She thought of the coldness in her wrinkled hands. She thought of the wind in her loud voice. She thought of the softness of her white hair. She thought of the gentleness of her touch. For the first time in her life, Michelin realized that Grandma Levy was like the first snow of winter.